A Place Called Dead

KIDS HAVE *TROUBLES* TOO

A House Between Homes:
Kids in the Foster Care System

What's Going to Happen Next?
Kids in the Juvenile Court System

I Live in Two Homes:
Adjusting to Divorce and Remarriage

When My Brother Went to Prison

When Daddy Hit Mommy

My Feelings Have Names

I Don't Keep Secrets

I Like Me

When Life Makes Me Mad

A Place Called Dead

When My Sister Got Sick

When My Dad Lost His Job

Sometimes My Mom Drinks Too Much

A Place Called Dead

by Sheila Stewart and Rae Simons

Mason Crest Publishers

MASON CREST PUBLISHERS INC.
370 Reed Road
Broomall, Pennsylvania 19008
(866)MCP-BOOK (toll free)
www.masoncrest.com

First Printing
9 8 7 6 5 4 3 2 1

Library of Congress Cataloging-in-Publication Data

Stewart, Sheila, 1975–
  A place called dead / by Sheila Stewart and Rae Simons.
       p. cm. — (Kids have troubles too)
  Includes index.
  ISBN (set) 978-1-4222-1691-0   ISBN 978-1-4222-1701-6
  ISBN (ppbk set) 978-1-4222-1904-1   ISBN 978-1-4222-1914-0 (pbk.)
  1. Death—Juvenile literature. 2. Death—Psychological aspects—Juvenile literature. I. Simons, Rae, 1957– II. Title.
  HQ1073.3.S744 2011
  155.9'37--dc22
                                          2010029366
Design by MK Bassett-Harvey.
Produced by Harding House Publishing Service, Inc.
www.hardinghousepages.com
Illustrations by Russell Richardson, RxDx Productions.
Cover design by Torque Advertising + Design.
Printed in USA by Bang Printing.

Introduction

Each child is unique—and each child encounters a unique set of circumstances in life. Some of these circumstances are more challenging than others, and how a child copes with those challenges will depend in large part on the other resources in her life.

The issues children encounter cover a wide range. Some of these are common to almost all children, including threats to self-esteem, anger management, and learning to identify emotions. Others are more unique to individual families, but problems such as parental unemployment, a death in the family, or divorce and remarriage are common but traumatic events in many children's lives. Still others— like domestic abuse, alcoholism, and the incarceration of a family member—are unfortunately not uncommon in today's world.

Whatever problems a child encounters in life, understanding that he is not alone is a key component to helping him cope. These books, both their fiction and nonfiction elements, allow children to see that other children are in the same situations. The books make excellent tools for triggering conversation in a nonthreatening way. They will also promote understanding and compassion in children who may not be experiencing these issues themselves.

These books offer children important factual information—but perhaps more important, they offer hope.

—Cindy Croft, M.A., Ed., Director of the Center for Inclusive Child Care

Ella could smell the cinnamon as soon as she opened the door to Grammy Jo's apartment. Grammy Jo had told Ella she simmered the cinnamon on the stove to make the whole apartment smell nice. None of the other apartments in the senior living complex seemed as friendly and happy as Grammy Jo's.

"Is that you, Ella?" Grammy Jo called out. "I'm in the living room."

Ella walked around the corner and found Grammy Jo sitting on her couch, working on a laptop that sat on a low table in front of her.

"Hi, Grammy Jo," Ella said, going over to sit next to her. "How's your book?"

"It's going well. Although Clara seems to be falling in love with John."

Clara was the heroine of the novel Grammy Jo was writing, and John was her flight instructor. Clara was training to be a pilot so she could become a WASP—a Women Air Force Service Pilot—which was what Grammy Jo had done when she was young, during World War II.

"Clara can't fall in love with John!" Ella objected. "She's supposed to marry David."

"She will," Grammy Jo said. "This is just a little side trip she's taking. Those happen, you know, in stories and in real life." She closed the laptop and put her arm around Ella. "Would you like some hot chocolate?"

"Sure." Ella stood up and put her hand out to help Grammy Jo up. She loved coming to visit Grammy Jo. She'd been coming at least twice a week for as long as she could remember. This spring her mom was teaching a late class at the university on Wednesdays, and her dad never got home before six anyway. Her mom had arranged for the school bus to drop Ella off at the senior apartments on Wednesdays.

Grammy Jo's pen rolled off the little table and Grammy Jo leaned down to pick it up before Ella had a chance, scraping her wrist on the side of the table.

"Ouch!" Grammy Jo said, looking down at the scrape, which was beginning to bleed a little.

"Are you okay?" Ella asked.

"Of course I am," Grammy Jo said. "Why don't you run get me a bandage while I start the hot chocolate."

"Tell me a story about when you were young," Ella asked, once they were sitting on the couch again and sipping hot chocolate. Grammy Jo told wonderful stories. She had left home when she was nineteen and become a pilot, flying planes across the United States during the war. After the war, the air force had sent her home, along with all the other women pilots. She'd wanted to keep flying, but instead she'd gotten married and had a baby— Ella's grandmother, who had died before Ella was born—and then worked as a kindergarten teacher for almost fifty years.

"I still miss flying," she said to Ella, sighing. "Ben—my husband, your great-grandpa—paid someone to take me up once, about thirty years ago. But it wasn't the same at all. I loved feeling the plane do what I wanted it to do. I felt free when I was flying."

She put her arm around Ella again and started telling her a story about one time when she had

flown into a thunderstorm. "I thought I wasn't going to make it that time," she said. "But I did. After I landed, I crawled out of my plane and lay on the tarmac. I was so surprised I wasn't dead. All the joy of being alive just bubbled up inside me and I started laughing, lying there on the ground with the rain running into my eyes."

"Were you scared to fly again after that?" Ella asked.

Grammy Jo looked thoughtful. "No," she said. "I knew I might be killed—some of my friends died in flight accidents—but I loved it so much that the risk was worth it. You could die at any time, but you shouldn't let that stop you from living."

The next day, in school, Ella's teacher, Ms. Wilson started teaching the class about poetry. "Poems can be funny or serious or sad," she said. "In just a few words, the poet makes us feel something."

"We're going to be writing our own poems," Ms. Wilson said. "So your homework tonight will be to think about what you might want to write about. Come up with a few ideas. You can start writing if you like, but we'll talk more about it tomorrow."

On the bus ride home, Ella thought about the poem. She'd had an idea right away about what she wanted to write about. She wanted to write about Grammy Jo being a pilot.

After supper, Ella worked on her poem, sitting curled up in the big chair in the living room.

"What are you writing?" Dad asked. He tried to look over her shoulder, but she put her hand over the paper.

"It's for school," she said. "I have to write a poem, but I don't want to show you until it's done."

"Okay," he said, smiling at her. "I look forward to reading it."

By the time Ella went to bed, she had written six lines. She thought the poem might be done, but she wasn't sure if Ms. Wilson would agree or not.

She had written:

When she flies, she is free
And she never wants to land.
When she's over the clouds,
She is happy and her heart is quiet,
Even though her plane is so loud
She sometimes thinks the wings might fall off.

The next morning when her mom came to wake her up, Ella knew right away something was wrong. Mom's eyes were all red and puffy, like she'd been crying.

"What happened?" Ella asked, sitting up. "What's wrong?"

Mom put her arms around Ella and hugged her. "It's Grammy Jo," she said.

"What about Grammy Jo?" Ella was afraid to hear what Mom would say.

"She . . . she . . . They think that she had a heart attack during the night." Mom gulped, as though a sob was trying to get out of her mouth. "Ella, Grammy Jo died last night."

"No." Ella shook her head. Then she said it again, but louder this time, "No! That can't be true. Because she was fine when I saw her. Maybe they're mixed up and it was somebody else who died." Her chest felt funny, as though something hard was growing inside there, something big and awful and jagged. "Call her, Mom! Call Grammy Jo and she'll tell you it's not true!"

"I wish it wasn't true," Mom said, holding Ella tighter. "I really wish it wasn't."

When her mom finally went downstairs again, Ella curled up in bed again and pulled the blanket over her head. She wished she could go to sleep again and wake up and this would all be a terrible dream. She couldn't sleep, though, and she knew it probably wasn't a dream.

Finally, she got up and got dressed. Mom was on the phone when she went out into the kitchen. She smiled at Ella, but Ella could see that tears kept running down her cheeks.

Ella didn't want to eat. She didn't want to do anything. She just wanted Grammy Jo to be still alive. She sat at the kitchen table with her head on her arms and waited for Mom to get off the phone.

The rest of the day went by in little quick jerks followed by long, long stretches when time seemed to stop moving. Ella didn't go to school. Instead, she went with Mom to the funeral home and sat in a fancy office while the funeral director talked to Mom. They talked about when the funeral would be and what kind of casket Grammy Jo would have and where she would be buried. Ella tried not to listen. She didn't want to think about Grammy Jo being put in the ground.

Then they went home again, and Mom called person after person to tell them Grammy Jo was dead. Ella hated hearing that word over and over. Dead wasn't a word that made sense with Grammy Jo.

After hearing Mom say the same things about ten times, though, Ella started getting mad. She didn't really know why she was mad, but she wanted Mom to stop talking about Grammy Jo like she didn't exist anymore. She ran down the hall to her room and slammed the door. She picked up a shoe that was lying on the floor and flung it as hard as she could against the wall. Then she threw herself onto her bed, put her head under the pillow, and yelled as loudly as she could.

A minute later, Mom knocked on the door. "Ella?"

"Grammy Jo is not supposed to be dead!" Ella screamed.

"She was very old, honey," Mom said. "But it's never easy when somebody we love dies."

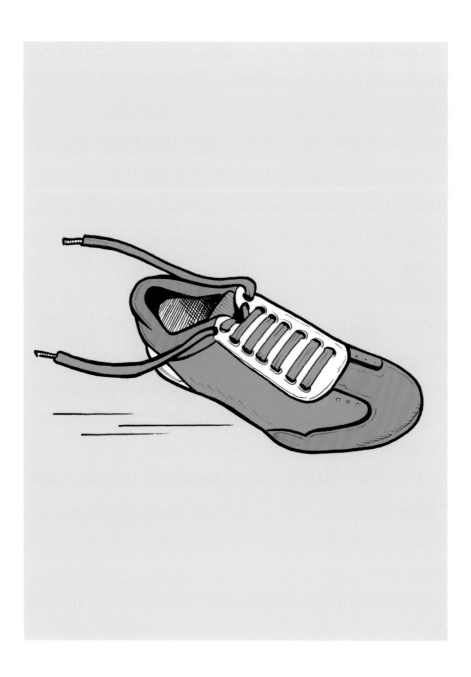

"But she didn't even get a chance to finish her novel," Ella said. "It isn't fair!" The thought of the novel that Grammy Jo had worked so hard on and was now never going to be finished was suddenly too much for Ella. All the tears that hadn't come out all day because she hadn't really believed Grammy Jo could really be dead were suddenly all fighting to get out at once. She buried her head in Mom's lap and sobbed.

Mom stroked her hair. "No, it's not fair," she said, and she was crying too. "I don't want her to be dead either."

"Then why do you keep calling people to tell them she's dead?"

"I have to. I have to let her family and friends know. And I need to let them know when the funeral is."

"Is there any way to change it?" Ella asked desperately. "Some way for her not to be dead after all?"

"Oh kiddo, I wish there was," Mom said. "People have been wishing that forever."

"I was writing her a poem," Ella said, and that started her sobbing all over again.

Things hadn't gotten any better by Monday, when the funeral was taking place. More people were around—aunts and uncles and cousins who had come for the funeral—but they were laughing and talking, as though they weren't as sad as Ella was, and that made Ella wish they weren't there at all.

When Ella and her parents walked into the room the funeral home had ready for them, the first thing Ella saw was a big picture of Grammy Jo on a stand. Aunt Melissa was next to it, setting up another stand, this one covered with pictures of Grammy Jo at different times during her life.

Ella was about to go over and look at the pictures, when something at the other end of the room distracted her. She turned her head and saw Grammy

Jo lying in a box. She gasped and ran toward her. Even now she was still thinking that maybe it had all been a mistake. Maybe Grammy Jo would sit up and smile at her and tell her it would all be okay.

Uncle Ryan was standing next to Grammy Jo. "She looks good, doesn't she?" he said to Ella. "Almost like she's just asleep."

But Ella didn't think she looked good. She stared down at Grammy Jo. Her white hair had been carefully curled and styled, and she was wearing a lot of makeup. Ella had never seen Grammy Jo look like that before. She put out one finger and touched the curls; they were stiff with hairspray. Her mouth was dark red with thick lipstick. Grammy Jo would have been horrified. She'd always said that she preferred to look natural.

Ignoring Uncle Ryan, Ella reached in again and put her hand in Grammy Jo's. Her hand was cold and stiff; it didn't seem like a person's hand at all, let alone Grammy Jo's. Ella leaned closer and sniffed, hoping to catch Grammy Jo's cinnamon smell, but she smelled strange and unfamiliar.

Maybe, Ella thought, it wasn't really Grammy Jo at all. Maybe somebody had made a big doll that looked like her instead. But then she saw the mark on Grammy Jo's wrist where she had scraped it on the table on Wednesday. Somebody had tried to cover it with makeup, but Ella could still see the mark. That meant it really did have to be Grammy Jo.

"Ella?" Uncle Ryan said. "I'm not sure you should be touching her. . . ."

Ella ignored him and walked over to where her mom had left her purse sitting beside a chair. She searched through the purse until she found her mom's lipstick, then grabbed a few tissues from a box on a table, and walked back to Grammy Jo's body. Uncle Ryan had walked away and was talking to some people Ella didn't know. She was glad he had left, even though he was usually one of her favorite uncles.

Leaning into the box—the casket, that was what it was called, she remembered now—Ella used the tissues to carefully wipe off as much of the red-pink lipstick as she could. She tried to wipe off some of the other makeup too, but the lipstick was what bothered her the most. When she had gotten off what she could, she stuffed the tissues into her pocket and opened her mom's lipstick. Mom's lipstick was shimmery, a browny-pink. If Grammy Jo had to wear lipstick—and she had to now to cover up the rest of that dark red-pink lipstick—then she would have liked this color much better. As carefully as she could, Ella put the lipstick on Grammy Jo's lips. She smudged it in a few places, so she took out the tissues again to fix it. She thought Grammy Jo looked a little better, and she wondered if she should do something about her hair next.

"Ella," Mom said from behind her, "what are you doing?"

Ella turned around, and Mom looked in at Grammy Jo, then back to Ella.

"I was fixing her makeup," Ella said.

Mom didn't say anything for a minute. She glanced down at Ella's hand. "Is that my lipstick?" she asked.

Ella handed it to her. "She looked terrible, Mom," she said. "Did you see her? She would have been so mad." Ella started to cry. "I wanted to do something for her, Mom. I wanted to show her we still love her, even though she's dead."

Mom put her arms around Ella and held her. She didn't say anything, just kissed the top of Ella's head.

For the rest of the time before the funeral started, Ella sat on the floor in a corner, behind an armchair. People came and sat in the armchair and never noticed she was there. She put her head down on her knees and thought about Grammy Jo. She thought about Grammy Jo saying, "You could die at any time, but you shouldn't let that stop you from living." Some of Grammy Jo's friends had died when they were really young, when their planes crashed, but Grammy Jo had lived until she was old. She had kept on being alive and being happy about it, even though she hadn't gotten to fly again and even though she'd had trouble walking when she got older.

Maybe, Ella thought, wherever she was now, she was flying an airplane. Maybe she was happy. She thought of Grammy Jo in a weird place called Dead, flying her plane and laughing.

When the funeral started, Mom made Ella come out from behind the chair. Ella sat between her parents and put her head on her mom's shoulder. She half listened as different people stood up and said nice things about Grammy Jo. Ella had always loved Grammy Jo, but she didn't know so many other people had too.

For the rest of the day, Ella tried to stay out of the way. She didn't want to talk to anybody. She just felt sad. From the funeral home, they had gone to the cemetery, where they buried Grammy Jo in the ground. That was bad. Ella tried not to think about Grammy Jo in a box under the ground. "That's not really her," she thought over and over again. "She's not there. She's in a place called Dead flying an airplane."

For the next few weeks, Ella told herself the same thing a lot. She missed Grammy Jo. When Wednesdays came and she went to her mom's office instead of Grammy Jo's apartment, she felt like the world was all wrong.

"I have to meet with a student," Mom said, the second Wednesday after Grammy Jo had died, "so I'm going to be right across the hall. You sit here and do your homework."

Ella sighed and sat down at her mom's desk. She opened her social studies book, but she couldn't make herself think about George Washington. Instead, she turned the pages of her notebook to

the page where she had written the poem about Grammy Jo.

After a moment, Ella picked up her pencil. She wrote:

For a long time, she doesn't get to fly anymore,
Even though life goes on.
But in her heart there's a little place where she is always flying
And always free.
Finally, when everyone else thinks it's too late for her,
She flies away to a place called Dead.
And now she is always flying, always happy, always free.

Ella put down her pencil and read what she had written. She thought Grammy Jo would like it. She would hug Ella and Ella would smell the cinnamon and she would tell Ella she was proud of her. Ella thought of the unfinished novel again and how sad that was. One day, she decided, she would finish Grammy Jo's novel herself. And Grammy Jo would be proud of that, too.

Dying Is a Part of Life

Everyone dies. That doesn't mean that death is easier to deal with, or that people understand death, but it does mean that it's a natural part of being a human being.

Most of the time, people who die are older. Ella's Grammy Jo was her great-grandmother, and she was probably in her 80s or 90s. These days, it's not uncommon for people to live even into their 100s! But sometimes, younger people die because they're sick, or because of an accident. Doctors work to make them better, but they're just too sick or hurt to get better. No matter when someone dies, it's always hard on the people who loved him or her. Young or old, it doesn't matter, because friends and family will miss the person who's gone.

What Is Death?

Death is the result of the body not working. Our bodies weren't made to last forever. Sooner or later they wear down and stop functioning. Once all parts of the body stop working, then a person is dead.

Death is more than a physical change, though. Nobody really knows exactly what happens when we die.

Some people think we have **souls** that go to heaven or are reborn, and others think that nothing happens. There are all sorts of answers, including religious ones, but the truth is that it's a mystery. That's part of what makes death so scary sometimes. No one gets to come back and tell us what happens after death!

Learning About Death

When you're really, really little, you probably aren't very aware of death. You're more concerned with eating, sleeping, and starting to explore the world. As you get a little older, you're slowly introduced to the idea of death through television, movies, adults' conversations, books, or personal experience. It's hard for little kids to understand death, and they might think it's just temporary. In other words, they may think that Grandpa is dead today—but next week, he'll come back, and things will go back to normal. Children think like that because they've never experienced anyone who goes away and never comes back.

By now, you probably know that death is permanent. No amount of wishing or hoping will bring the

Understand the Word

Souls are the spiritual part of a person, not the physical body. Some people think that souls go on existing after the body dies.

We know what happens to our physical bodies once they die, but the rest of what happens after death is a mystery.

person who died back, even though he or she will always live in your memory. Knowing someone who died makes you learn about death pretty fast. Even if you know the facts about death, you don't really start to understand until you come face-to-face with it. The death of family members, friends, or pets is very sad, but it can also be a good time to ask all the questions you have about death. You won't get all the answers, but you'll start to learn about it and come to terms with it. That's something that every human being who has ever lived has had to do.

Grieving

There's no avoiding the fact that people are sad when someone they care about dies. Someone we depend on and love has always been there—and suddenly she's not. The process by which we cope with a death is called grieving or mourning. There are lots of different ways of grieving, and they change from **culture** to culture. In our culture, we usually have a funeral for the dead person and bury him in the ground or we may **cremate** him.

Understand the Word

A group of people who share the same customs, language, and beliefs make up a **culture**.

To **cremate** a body means to burn it and turn it into ashes, which can be scattered. Cremation is an alternative to burial.

Other people expect friends and family to be sad, to cry, and to be angry or confused for a period of time.

The process of grieving can be pretty long. First comes shock, when we first hear that someone is dead. We might not be able to believe it or we could think it's a trick, like Ella did. Then comes a whole bunch of other emotions. You can be sad, upset, angry, frustrated, or guilty; all of these emotions are normal and are part of the process of grieving.

Understand the Word

Resentment is a type of deep anger because you feel that something is unfair.

More About Those Feelings

If someone you love dies, you'll probably feel lots of different things. You will obviously be sad about the death, if you were close to the person that died, but you might not cry for a while, even if you think you should. Not being able to cry is a common experience for grieving people, but it might make you frustrated or guilty. You could also feel frustration because you think death isn't fair. It's not fair that someone you loved was taken away from you and can't do the things she enjoyed anymore! Maybe you even feel anger and **resentment** at the person who died. How dare he die and leave you behind to face all the changes that his death brings? Many people feel guilty that they're still alive while the dead person isn't. Remember, it's not your fault that your grandma, brother, or family friend died. Finally, fear is also a common feeling when someone dies. You start to think that other people you love could die at any time, or that you could die soon, too.

Changes

Feelings aren't the only things that change. Schedules are one of the most obvious things that are different. Ella used to go to her Grammy Jo's apartment after school twice a week, but after she died, she had to go to her mom's office. It seems like just a little change, but Ella was lonely at the office, and it reminded her that her great-grandmother was gone. Changes in how you live your life are hard anyway, but when they remind you that someone died, they can be even harder.

Death can affect you in other ways, too. Some people have trouble sleeping, and have nightmares that wake them up during the middle of the night. Kids who have had an experience with death might also end up doing poorly in school for a while, either because they have missed some school or because they are too sad or confused to focus on schoolwork properly.

Your bad feelings can also turn into feeling sick. If you're worried and sad all the time, your body knows it. All those emotions can give you headaches, stomachaches, or other problems. They aren't fake, so take care of them like you would any other illness, but you should also deal with your grief so that both your mind and your body feel better.

How to Mourn

That's a lot of bad things that can happen to you while you grieve! But don't worry– you probably won't feel all of those things all at once, and they go away after a while. Grieving is temporary, and only lasts for a little while. Pretty soon, you learn how to go on with your life. That doesn't mean you forget the person that died; it just means that you keep them in your heart but go on living, which the dead person would certainly want you to do.

There are lots of things you can do to mourn in a healthy way, and eventually move on. First, let all your emotions out. If you're angry, hit a pillow or dance

After someone dies, people experience lots of emotions during the grieving process. You could be sad, angry, or frustrated, or feel all of these things at once.

around to loud music (but don't take your anger out at other people). If you're really sad, let yourself cry as hard as you want. After a while, start looking at pictures or videos of the person who died, if you think it will help you. Keep something with you that reminds you of that person, like a necklace or a little **trinket**. Eventually, you might want to visit the grave of the person who died. Whatever helps you feel better is okay. Things that help some people may not help others, so be honest with the rest of your family about what helps you and what doesn't—and respect the things that help them feel better even if they're different from what you're experiencing.

Writing and being creative is also a great way to let out your emotions and learn to heal. Keep a journal, write poems like Ella, paint what you're feeling, or draw pictures of the person who died.

Talking is the best way for a lot of people to grieve, though sometimes people also need times alone to work things out themselves. Talk to your parents, your siblings, a religious leader, your friends, or anyone else you're close to. Your friends especially might be a lit-

Understand the Word

A **trinket** is any small item that has no particular use. Charms, small toys, or souvenirs can all be considered trinkets.

tle nervous to talk to you at first, because they don't know what to expect. Once they see that you just need someone to talk with, they'll likely be more than happy to sit down with you.

Another good person to talk to is your school counselor. If you'd rather talk to someone not personally affected by the death, or if you'd just like to talk to someone who knows how to deal with these issues, then a counselor is the perfect choice. Almost every school has a counselor who has been specially trained to listen to students' problems and help them work through them. Ask your teacher or another adult at school how you can set up an appointment with a counselor.

What to Expect at a Funeral

Pretty soon after a death, there will be a funeral. If you've never been to a funeral, like Ella hadn't, a funeral can be confusing and a little scary. All funerals are different, especially if the funeral service is religious. Some funerals happen within a day of the death, some have open caskets so that you can see the **deceased**

> ### *Understand the Word*
>
> Someone who is **deceased** is no longer alive. It's a less direct way of describing someone as dead.

person, and some are huge affairs with hundreds of people. There are a few things you can expect from almost all funerals though. The dead person is celebrated by those still living, and speeches are given about their life. The service is usually followed by a trip to the cemetery, where the dead person is lowered into the ground. This might not be the case if the person chose to be cremated, though, and in that case, the ashes might be scattered somewhere the person loved. Other times, ashes are kept in a special container in the family's home.

When something is celebrated, people think about all the good happy things about that thing. If you celebrate Christmas, for instance, you honor that day by making it special in various ways, from decorations to special foods to gifts. If you celebrate someone's life, you spend time thinking about and honoring all the good things about that person. This might also include the person's favorite songs, eating a special meal, or looking at pictures of the person.

Understand the Word

Customs with set rules and parts are called **rituals**. Other examples of rituals include weddings and graduations. Rituals are more or less the same within a culture, so most funerals in our culture share a lot of the same rules and characteristics.

Sometimes people say that funerals aren't for the dead, they're for the living. Funerals are **rituals** that help people say goodbye. Family and friends know that there are lots of people there who cared about the dead person, and they can all grieve together for a little while.

It's helpful to go to your grandpa's or your cousin's funeral, even if you're a little afraid. Your parents should make sure you know what will happen beforehand, and if there are any ways you can help out. If you absolutely don't want to go, then you should talk about it with your parents. It will be important to other people that you're there—and you may be surprised to find that it actually helps you feel a little better.

Understand the Word

A **life span** is how long a living thing can expect to be alive, on average. Dogs' and cats' life spans are around 15 years, while human life spans can be 80 to 90 years.

When a Pet Dies

It's hard when a person dies, but what about a pet? Cats, dogs, hamsters, and fish are all part of the family, so it makes sense that you'll be sad when they die. Pets have a shorter **life span** than humans, so their deaths are often the first experience kids have with death. Maybe your dog died a couple years ago, or you've had several fish you've had to flush down the toilet or bury in the backyard. Even though they're not humans, pets are hard to say goodbye to, too.

Other people don't always understand why you're so upset about a pet's death. But you know that your animal loved you no matter what, and that he was always there for you. It's okay to be upset, and you can grieve for an animal just like for people. Use some of the same techniques to get over a pet's death, like writing down your feelings, talking to someone, and remembering your pet in small ways.

Worried About Death

It only makes sense that you'll be thinking more about death if someone you're close to dies. What if your mom or dad dies next, you may wonder? What if your friend dies? What if you die? These are reasonable questions, but don't dwell on them too much. Life involves risk; if you never did anything, then you wouldn't have a very good life. But most of the time, people are very much alive, and will be around for a long time. If you let fear of death take over your life, then you won't be happy and you won't have much of a life.

Talk to your family about your worries. Everyone has worried about death from time to time, and they can help you sort out your own worries. Your family can't help you if you don't tell them what's wrong!

Don't Be Afraid to Ask Questions

Death doesn't have to be so mysterious, scary, and confusing. No one knows all the answers about death, but adults do know a lot. You'll probably have lots of questions the first time someone you know dies, so don't be afraid to ask them. Being confused about death will only mean that the grieving process takes longer, and that you won't understand death the next time you have to deal with it. It's better to ask your questions now, and start to understand what death is and how we as people live with it. Pretty soon, you'll feel more comfortable with death, even if it still makes you sad.

Questions to Think About

1. Everyone believes different things about death. No one knows all the answers for sure, but beliefs about death can be comforting. What do YOU think happens when a person dies?

2. How did you feel when Ella put different lipstick on Grammy Jo's dead body? Why did you feel that way? Why do you think Ella did that? Was it a good thing for her to do? Why or why not?

3. How do you think Ella will feel about Grammy Jo after a year has passed? How do you think she will feel about Grammy Jo when she has grown up? Do you think she will ever forget her?

4. When someone dies, people often say that person lives on through the people who loved her or him. What do you think that means? How will Grammy Jo continue to live in Ella? Have you ever experienced this?

Further Reading

Jones, Diane. *Coping with Death: Saying Goodbye.* New York: Amazon, 2010.

Mundy, Michaelene. *Sad Isn't Bad: A Good-Grief Guidebook for Kids Dealing with Loss.* St. Meinrad, Ind.: 2001.

Wolfelt, Alan D. *Healing Your Grieving Heart: 100 Practical Ideas.* New York: Companion Press, 2001.

Find Out More on the Internet

Death and Grief
kidshealth.org/teen/your_mind/emotions/someone_died.html

Working Through Loss
www.cyh.com/HealthTopics/HealthTopicDetailsKids.
aspx?p=335&np=287&id=1789

The websites listed on this page were active at the time of publication. The publisher is not responsible for websites that have changed their address or discontinued operation since the date of publication. The publisher will review and update the websites upon each reprint.

Index

anger 34, 36, 38

casket 16, 23, 39
counselor 39
cremation 33, 40
crying 14, 19, 24, 34, 38
culture 33, 40

doctor 30

fear 35, 42
feelings 34–36, 38, 42

funeral 16, 19–20, 24–25, 33, 39–41

grieving 33–34, 36, 38, 41–43

pets 33, 41–42

talking 38–39, 41–43

worry 36, 42–43
writing 13–14, 20, 28, 38, 42

Picture Credits

Elenathewise; fotolia: p. 32
September, Jane; fotolia: p. 37

To the best knowledge of the publisher, all images not specifically credited are in the public domain. If any image has been inadvertently uncredited, please notify Harding House Publishing Service, 220 Front Street, Vestal, New York 13850, so that credit can be given in future printings.

About the Authors

Sheila Stewart has written several dozen books for young people, both fiction and nonfiction, although she especially enjoys writing fiction. She has a master's degree in English and now works as a writer and editor. She lives with her two children in a house overflowing with books, in the Southern Tier of New York State.

Rae Simons is a freelance author who has written numerous educational books for children and young adults. She also has degrees in psychology and special education, and she has worked with children encountering a range of troubles in their lives.

About the Consultant

Cindy Croft, M.A. Ed., is Director of the Center for Inclusive Child Care, a state-funded program with support from the McKnight Foundation, that creates, promotes, and supports pathways to successful inclusive care for all children. Its goal is inclusion and retention of children with disabilities and behavioral challenges in community child care settings. Cindy Croft is also on the faculty at Concordia University, where she teaches courses on young children with special needs and the emotional growth of young children. She is the author of several books, including *The Six Keys: Strategies for Promoting Children's Mental Health.*